Morris Kumpel
and the Wings
of Icarus

Morris Rumpel and the Wings of Icarus

Betty Waterton

A Groundwood Book

Douglas & McIntyre

TORONTO/VANCOUVER

Canadian Cataloguing in Publication Data

Waterton, Betty
  Morris Rumpel and the wings of Icarus

ISBN 0-88899-099-5

I. Title.

PS8595.A73M67 1989   jC813'.54 C89-094754-6
PZ7.W37Mo 1989

Groundwood Books/Douglas & McIntyre Ltd.
26 Lennox Street, Third Floor
Toronto, Ontario M6G 1J4

Design by Michael Solomon
Cover illustration by Eric Beddows

Printed and bound in Canada

1 2 3 4 5 6 7 8 9 6 5 4 3 2 1 0 9 8

To Claude,
who was also born to fly.

1

As Quincy Rumpel clumped up the front steps of her house, the door suddenly flew open.

"Guess what!" cried Morris, her younger brother. "Guess what I'm going to do tomorrow?"

"I couldn't care less," Quincy answered grumpily. She had just finished doing her paper route, and she was feeling hot and out of sorts. She pushed past him, grateful to reach the cool dimness of the Rumpel front hall.

"I'm going on a plane, that's what! I'm going to visit Grandma and Grandpa at Rumpel Ranch, by myself, that's what!"

Quincy stopped in her tracks and stared at her brother. "Get out of here."

"I am so. Ask Mom."

"I don't believe it. Where is Mom, anyway?"

Just then a sort of muffled hum was heard coming from the living-room. "Mmm-mm-mmmmm, mmmmm."

Peering in, Quincy saw a figure sitting on the chesterfield, hunched intently over something.

"Mom? Is that you?"

Her mouth bristling with pins, Mrs. Rumpel wiggled her fingers briefly. Then she resumed tugging at a needle that was stuck fast in some bright-pink material on her lap.

"What's with Morris going on the plane to Grandma's? Tell me it isn't true." Quincy flopped down on the other end of the chesterfield. "I don't think I feel so good," she added, kicking off her sneakers.

"It's true! It's true!" shouted Morris. "I am so going! All by myself!"

Quincy glared at him.

Mrs. Rumpel took the pins out of her mouth. "Grandpa sent him a plane ticket to visit them. Isn't that nice? He says he needs someone to help him with something."

"But I'm the oldest!" cried Quincy. "Why not me?"

"I guess they knew you were busy with your paper route, and Leah would get too homesick if she went. . . . Did you say you weren't feeling well?" Mrs. Rumpel reached over and felt her daughter's forehead.

"I'm okay," said Quincy, brushing her mother's hand away. "I'm just sick of my paper route, and *I* could use a holiday somewhere, that's all. . . . Hey, that's a neat sweatshirt. I could tie-dye it. Whose is it?"

"Morris's. He picked it out himself. He didn't have anything to wear on the plane, so. . . . Oh! We almost forgot your haircut, Morris!" Jumping to her feet, Mrs. Rumpel called out to her husband, "Harvey, don't forget about Morris's haircut!"

"Too late!" answered Mr. Rumpel cheerfully from his office behind the stairs. "The barber's closed by now."

"But he looks like a little old hippie! You'll have to take him to the beauty parlour in the mall, that's all. They're open late."

"The beauty parlour?!" howled Morris as his father propelled him towards the door. "But my hair doesn't even need cutting! It's just getting right . . ."

As her brother's wails faded away into the distance, Quincy watched her mother mending a small tear in the neck of the pink sweatshirt. "Mom, did you snip the material again?"

"It's these darn scissors." Mrs. Rumpel stared bleakly at her puckered repair job.

"Nobody but us has all their labels snipped out, you know. You don't really have to do that."

"Some of them are scratchy. Anyway, it's done now." Stuffing her pins and needles away in the cookie tin that served as a sewing basket, Mrs. Rumpel headed for the kitchen. Quincy straggled after her.

The table was heaped with freshly washed laundry—most of it Morris's. Mrs. Rumpel began sorting everything into five piles.

Suddenly she held up a handful of small, saggy underpants. "Look at these!" she cried. "Morris's elastic is all shot."

"So?" said Quincy, spreading peanut butter on the end of a banana. "Who's going to see them, except Grandma?"

"But he can't go on the plane with these! What if something happened? One of us will just have to go to the mall and buy him some new underwear . . ."

"Don't look at me. I'd sooner die!"

"Then I'll have to go myself, and right away, before the stores close. Supper's practically ready. There's some leftover pasta in the fridge, and some spaghetti sauce in the freezer. And, Quincy, would you please finish sorting this laundry. We have to get Morris packed up tonight."

"Oh, sure! And perhaps his royal highness

would like a stretch limo to take him to the airport tomorrow?"

"I could use a limo right now," said her mother, putting on her jogging shoes. Then she set out on foot for the mall, since Mr. Rumpel and Morris had taken the car.

A few minutes later, Leah came in from her baton-twirling class. Humming happily and twirling an imaginary baton, she strutted into the kitchen. There she found her older sister sitting at the table, grimly sorting socks. On the counter was a large empty bowl with a few shreds of cold spaghetti stuck to its sides. Beside it was a frosty-looking yogurt container with "S.S." marked on it with black crayon.

"Sugared strawberries?" asked Leah hopefully, popping off the lid.

"Spaghetti sauce," Quincy informed her. "Mom's special code. Did you know Morris is going on a holiday by himself to Grandma and Grandpa's tomorrow? On a plane, no less?"

"All by himself?" Leah made a face. "I don't think I'd like to go on a plane by myself. Where's Mom?"

"At the store. Buying Morris some new underwear, in case there's a plane crash or something."

"I sure wouldn't mind some new underwear. I haven't had any since Aunt Fan sent me the seven days of the week ones last Christmas. They're mostly all worn out—except for Saturday and Sunday."

"Why not Saturday and Sunday?"

"I think it's because I stay in my pyjamas longer on the weekends. What are we having for supper?"

Quincy fired some rolled-up balls of socks at the empty bowl on the counter. "We're supposed to be having spaghetti, but guess who ate all the noodles and then put the empty bowl back in the fridge. I sure hope Grandma knows what she's doing, inviting the Walking Mouth for a holiday."

"There must be more pasta somewhere!" Leah began opening and closing cupboard doors.

"Don't bother looking. I already did. There isn't."

"But what can we have? I'm starving!"

"Nyet problemy! Simplissimo! We'll have spaghetti sauce on toast. With a tossed salad. You can make the salad."

"And I suppose you'll make the toast?"

"You've got it, little sister!"

2

When Mrs. Rumpel returned from the store, she had three pairs of underpants and a new toothbrush for Morris, and a plum pudding wrapped in red cellophane.

"Plum pudding?" asked Leah. "Who eats plum pudding in the middle of the summer?"

"Grandpa does. He loves it. Besides, it was on sale. It will make a nice little present for Morris to take. Where is he, by the way? Aren't they back yet from the hairdresser's?"

"No," replied Quincy. "They probably had to anesthetize Morris first. He loves his hair."

At that moment the kitchen door opened, and Mr. Rumpel stomped in. "Don't ever ask me to take that boy to get his hair cut again!" he fumed.

"What did you do with him?" cried his wife. "Where is he?"

As she was speaking, Morris sidled in through the doorway, head lowered and shoulders hunched.

"Ta-*dah*!" cried Quincy. "Here he comes. Mr. Pre-teen Canada!"

"He doesn't look any different," said Leah.

Mrs. Rumpel looked at her husband accusingly. "Didn't you get it cut?"

"Oh, we got it cut, all right. Twelve dollars' worth!"

Mrs. Rumpel inspected the back of Morris's head. "I guess it does look a little better," she said finally. "But not much."

"They took off almost two centimetres!" moaned Morris. "Right where I needed it most!"

* * *

After a somewhat meagre meal of tomato-sauce-smeared toast and a lettuce-and-mayonnaise salad, Morris went upstairs to have a bath and organize his clothes. "But I'm not finished eating yet," he warned. "I'll be back!"

Mr. Rumpel was dispatched to the basement to look for the small blue suitcase with red stripes. "It's a nice light one," said his wife.

Mr. Rumpel was gone a long time. When he finally reappeared, he looked hot and dusty. He was lugging a large brown leather suitcase covered in old steamship labels. "Is this it?" he asked hopefully.

14

Mrs. Rumpel shook her head. "Good grief, no! That's the one Aunt Fan took on her cruise to Tierra del Fuego. Morris can't lug that around. I'll come down and help you look. You girls clean up the kitchen, please."

"You'd think Morris was taking off for the Olympics or something," grumbled Quincy, scooping leftovers into Snowflake's red rubber dog dish.

"Hey, watch where you're putting that stuff, Quince!" cried Leah, peeling a soggy crust of toast from her leg. "But wouldn't it be awful if Morris's plane really was hijacked? What if he actually did end up in some place like Tierra del Fuego?"

"Nobody's going to bother hijacking that plane. It's only going to Cranberry Corners. I just wish I was going, that's all. Besides, if anything did happen, I know some karate. *Pow! Pow! Bam!*" Making jabbing motions at the kitchen taps with her fists, Quincy kicked out vigorously behind her with her left leg, catching Leah on the seat.

"Quincy! Watch what you're doing!"

Just then Mrs. Rumpel emerged from the basement. "I knew it was there somewhere!" she said triumphantly. Behind her trailed Mr. Rumpel, looking hotter and dustier than before and carrying a small blue suitcase with a red stripe.

Suddenly a voice announced, "Here I come, everybody!" All heads swivelled towards the doorway as a figure in camouflage pyjamas staggered into the kitchen. On its back was a large old army backpack, complete with bed roll and dangling canteen.

"What's for chow?" asked Morris.

"You're certainly not going to Cranberry Corners like that!" said his mother. "Look, we found this nice little blue suitcase—"

"No way!" yelled Morris, clutching his shoulder straps.

"Don't you yell at me, young man!"

"I won't take a suitcase!"

"He's all packed, Mom," pleaded Leah.

"But . . . he can hardly walk with that thing!"

"Mom, nobody under twenty-five uses a suitcase," said Quincy. "Tell you what. I'll rent him my good hiking backpack. It's a lot lighter than this old thing."

"I'll have you know that 'this old thing' will be a valuable antique some day," muttered Mr. Rumpel, gazing fondly at his old equipment.

"I won't pay rent!" howled Morris.

Mrs. Rumpel sighed. "You may lend your

brother your backpack if you wish," she told Quincy. "But you will not rent it to him."

"Okay, but he'd better look after it," warned Quincy. "I'll need it when I go to Europe."

Her parents looked at her in surprise. "Europe? When are you going to Europe?"

"You know, after I graduate. When I save enough money. Gwen and I are going. I have forty-two dollars saved so far."

Morris hooted. "Forty-two dollars! By the time you've saved up enough, Chucky and I will have graduated, too, so we can all go together!"

Groaning, Quincy booted him out of the kitchen.

3

It was barely daylight the next morning when the silence of the sleeping Rumpel house was shattered by a shrill ringing.

"Fire! Fire!" screeched Leah, sitting bolt upright in bed.

"No fire. . . . Just alarm clocks . . ." said a sleepy voice from the other side of the room. Yanking the covers over her head, Quincy mumbled, "You know Dad always sets three of them when anybody's going anywhere . . ."

In a few moments, the door opened and Mrs. Rumpel appeared, dressed in her best polyester-and-cotton pantsuit. "Time to get up, girls! We don't want Morris to miss his plane!"

"But it doesn't go till nearly noon!" The blankets heaved as Quincy rose majestically to a sitting position. She was wearing rumpled pyjamas, tie-dyed by herself into a pattern of yellow splotches somewhat resembling fried eggs.

"Well, hurry along anyway. I have to go downstairs and make apple pancakes for breakfast. They're Morris's favourite."

A short while later, the girls joined their parents for Morris's farewell breakfast. The table was set with a pitcher of orange juice, a platter of pancakes and a large bouquet of nasturtiums.

"Oh, good," said Quincy. "Nasturtiums! That's what you get to eat sometimes in fancy restaurants." Nipping off several of the orange flowers, she began to nibble them.

"Don't eat any more," said her mother. "I want to send them to Grandma with Morris."

"Where is he, by the way?" Mr. Rumpel looked around the table.

"Didn't you call him?" asked Mrs. Rumpel. "I thought you did."

"I knew something would happen!" wailed Leah.

"Don't worry, I'll get him." Quincy pushed back her chair and stood up. "It will be my pleasure!" Munching a nasturtium and cackling under her breath, she strode off.

Before long, the Rumpels heard a loud howl coming from upstairs. Then Quincy reappeared, followed by a bleary-eyed Morris. Little rivulets of water were running down his face, and his hair was wet.

"She poured water on me!" he complained. "I was having a dream about driving a Ferrari up to Grandma's, and she poured water on me and woke me up!"

* * *

When breakfast was finished, Mr. Rumpel looked at his watch and announced, "All right, everybody. The car leaves for the airport in exactly five minutes!"

"Good grief, Dad! It's only eight o'clock," cried Quincy. "I'm not even dressed."

"You've got to give us more time, Harvey," insisted Mrs. Rumpel. "I haven't got my face on yet."

"I'm ready," said Morris, reaching for a leftover pancake that had been sitting on Quincy's plate. "As soon as I get dressed."

Mr. Rumpel looked at his watch. "All right. Ten minutes, then."

Leah was the first to reappear, wearing a blue denim skirt, white blouse and frilled socks. Sitting down on the front hall bench, she opened a horse magazine and proceeded to read it.

Mrs. Rumpel was next. Clutching a bouquet of nasturtiums and the plum pudding, she called up the stairs, "Morris! Quincy! Hurry up!"

"I'm coming!" came a muffled voice from the

landing. Mrs. Rumpel looked up and saw what appeared to be a pair of jeans locked in combat with a pink sweatshirt.

"Morris? Aren't you dressed yet?" she cried.

A tousled red head emerged above the sweatshirt. "It's me, Mom," said Quincy, bounding down the stairs.

"And just what are you doing in Morris's new sweatshirt?"

"It's all right. I traded him all my old comics for it. I don't read them anymore. Besides, this is a bit too big for Morris."

"He likes it big. Anyway, I bought it for him to wear to Grandma's, so give it back to him."

"But, Mom!" Quincy peered at herself in the hall mirror. "It's too pink for Morris." She fluffed out her recently permed and frizzy red hair.

"Give it *back*!" Mrs. Rumpel glared at her daughter.

Squirming out of the sweatshirt as she went, Quincy stomped upstairs. Halfway up she met Morris, who was on his way down. Draping the sweatshirt ungraciously over his head, she continued on her way.

Morris stuffed it into his backpack. He was wearing his black Harley-Davidson T-shirt.

"What happened to your sleeves?" cried his mother, staring in dismay at his ripped armholes.

"I took 'em out."

Leah glanced up from her magazine. "He looks kind of macho, Mom."

"Thanks," said Morris. "I think so, too."

"With that long hair, you look like nobody's child," moaned his mother. "Grandma and Grandpa won't even recognize you!"

"That reminds me," said Mr. Rumpel, appearing from his office behind the stairs. "I've got something for you." And he held out a flat white plastic pouch attached to a white strap.

"That's neat," said Morris. "What is it?"

"It's got your tickets in it, and all the information about who's going to meet you in Cranberry Corners, etcetera."

"It's like a little shoulder bag!" said Leah. "What does the 'U.M.' stand for?"

"That stands for 'Unaccompanied Minor.' "

"Which means 'Little Kid'!" said Quincy, clattering downstairs.

"I'll put it in my backpack," said Morris.

"No," said Mr. Rumpel. "You have to wear it around your neck. Like this . . ." And he looped it over Morris's head.

"No way! I'm not wearing it!"

"It covers up the motorcycle on his T-shirt, Dad," protested Leah.

"No matter," said Mr. Rumpel firmly. "It's airline policy."

"I think it's a good idea," said Mrs. Rumpel.

Morris stared at his reflection in the hall mirror. ''People will think I'm a baby or something!"

Quincy studied her little brother thoughtfully. "You know, it looks kind of like something the astronauts might wear — all white and everything. It's pretty neat, actually."

"Ummmm." Morris stuck out his chin and nudged the pouch slightly over to one side. "Maybe it is kind of neat . . ."

''And the 'U.M.' could stand for 'Ultra Macho'!" added Quincy, waving her arms dramatically. "Or even 'Utterly Ma—' "

"It's time to go, everybody!" Mr. Rumpel interrupted impatiently, and all the Rumpels scrambled for the door.

4

As he started the motor, Mr. Rumpel turned around and looked at Morris. "Now, are you sure you've got everything?"

"I could use some more money," said Morris hopefully.

"Wait!" cried Mrs. Rumpel, suddenly jumping out of the car. As she dashed back inside the house, her empty seat was promptly filled by the Rumpels' big white dog, Snowflake.

"Out! Out!" ordered Mr. Rumpel, shoving.

"Oh, let him come!" begged the back-seat chorus.

Refusing to budge, Snowflake remained with his large and furry rear end planted firmly in the middle of the front seat. In a few minutes Mrs. Rumpel returned, bearing the plum pudding, the bouquet of nasturtiums and Morris's soccer boots. When all attempts to drag Snowflake from the car failed, she squeezed in beside him.

"Here, we almost forgot these," she said, handing the boots and pudding to Morris. "It was lucky I found them. They were both at the back of your closet!"

"Ma, I don't have any room!"

"His backpack's full of comics," explained Leah.

"*My* comics!" said Quincy, yanking them out and stuffing in the boots and pudding.

"I didn't think there would be this much traffic so early," said Mr. Rumpel as they crawled along in the slow lane.

"Maybe you should try to get in the other lane," suggested Mrs. Rumpel from the other side of Snowflake.

"My stomach feels funny," said Morris.

"Dad, hurry! Before Morris throws up!" begged Quincy, leaning away from her brother.

Mr. Rumpel switched lanes, and they breezed along the freeway and through a tunnel.

"I didn't think we had to go through the tunnel to get to the airport," said Mrs. Rumpel.

"I just saw a sign that said 'Border Crossing,' " cried Quincy. "We're on our way to the States!"

Leah began to cry.

"I hope I don't miss my plane," said Morris, forgetting about his stomach.

"Find an exit!" ordered Mrs. Rumpel.

"Find an exit! Find an exit!" echoed Leah and Quincy.

Mr. Rumpel looked grim. "What do you think I'm looking for?" he asked.

* * *

When they finally reached the airport, it was almost Morris's boarding time. Leaving Snowflake in the car, the five Rumpels straggled hurriedly through the terminal building to the boarding gate. There they gathered in a little cluster to say goodbye to Morris.

Suddenly Quincy cried, "Wait!" and dashed away. In a few minutes she was back. "Here," she said, thrusting a chocolate bar into Morris's willing hands.

Mr. Rumpel tucked a five-dollar bill into his son's wallet, and some quarters into his pocket. "You should always have some quarters on you, in case you have to use a pay phone," he said gruffly.

Her eyes brimming with tears, Leah handed her horse magazine to her brother. "You can read it," she said. "But bring it back. I haven't finished it yet."

As he gasped for breath in his mother's tight hug, Morris was pleasantly surprised to feel another crisp bill and some more quarters being deposited in his pocket.

"We'll drive up and get you next month. Maybe sooner!" sniffled Mrs. Rumpel.

"Next month is only two weeks away," added Mr. Rumpel cheerfully.

Morris's throat felt tight, so he didn't say anything. He just gave a little wave. Then, grasping his nasturtiums, he walked through the gate into the boarding area.

"Look at his shoelaces!" sobbed Mrs. Rumpel. "They're all undone!"

"It's okay, Mom," Quincy told her. "That's the style."

The four Rumpels stood watching until Morris's blue backpack disappeared in the crowd. But just as they turned to leave, they heard an electronic beeper.

"That's the security scanner," said Mr. Rumpel. "Somebody got caught!"

"I thought I saw somebody carrying a funny-looking bundle!" Leah's eyes were wide with alarm.

"I'm going to find out about this!" said Quincy grimly, and she began wriggling her way through to the gate. In a few minutes, she was back.

27

"It was just Morris's plum pudding," she reported. "But they let him go. He's on his way now."

Leah breathed a sigh of relief, and the four Rumpels made their way back to their car. When they opened the door, Mrs. Rumpel let out a little gasp.

"Morris's oranges!" she cried, lifting up a plastic bag of four flattened oranges. "I forgot to give him these oranges to snack on. Snowflake must have been sitting on them."

"That's okay," said Quincy. "We'll eat 'em."

"Sometimes they're juicier when they're flat," said Leah.

And so, eating their oranges, they rode home. The ride was unusually quiet—for the Rumpels.

5

"**H**ere's your seat, Morris, right beside the window," said the stewardess. "Enjoy your flight to Cranberry Corners!"

"You know all about me!" Morris looked at her in surprise. *Wow!* he thought. *Are you ever beautiful!*

The stewardess smiled a dazzling smile. "We have to know about our special passengers," she said, stowing his backpack and the nasturtiums in the overhead compartment. "My goodness, this pack is really heavy!"

"Not for me. I've been working on my biceps lately." Morris flexed his arm to show her. He was just about to tell her about his body-building program, when a large lady with a knitting bag sat down beside him.

"I'll be seeing you later, Morris," said the stewardess. As she retreated before the swarm of advancing passengers, she winked. Morris blinked back.

In case such an opportunity arose again, he began to practise winking. But each time he tried it, he could see his nose twitch out of the corner of his eye, and feel his mouth open.

The large lady took some knitting out of her bag and began to knit on an afghan. As she knit, she gazed around her contentedly. Suddenly she noticed Morris's twitching face. "Are you all right, dear?" she asked. "Shall I call the attendant?"

"No, thanks," mumbled Morris. "I'm okay." Then he turned his face to the window and intently studied the top of the wing.

Feeling a little pang in his stomach, he remembered Quincy's chocolate bar. He pulled it out of his pocket and peeled back the paper. The chocolate was melting, so he ate it quickly. Then he opened Leah's horse magazine to an interesting-looking picture of some large worms. The article was called "How to Worm Your Pony." It was not as interesting as the picture.

The stewardess's voice came crackling through the plane. "Please make sure your seatbelts are fastened, in preparation for take-off!" *She sounds different on the intercom,* thought Morris. *More like my teacher!*

Click! Click! Click! All around him, people were clicking on their seatbelts. Groping frantically, Morris hunted, but he could only find one end of his. Suddenly he was filled with panic. He held up his arm and waved it.

"I haven't got one!" he cried.

The beautiful stewardess hurried down the aisle to help him, and the missing strap was quickly located. Morris had been sitting on it.

As the plane taxied to the runway, Morris turned his attention to the take-off. The motors revved, and the plane surged forward. *It's just like being in a Ferrari!* he thought, as they roared past the airport buildings.

Then all at once they were airborne and climbing. Morris's stomach went tight with excitement.

He stared out the window. Below him were little Monopoly houses and cars like Dinky toys. He couldn't tell which were trees and which were just bushes. They all looked the same from above! For a while he puzzled over tiny rectangles and ovals that shimmered like jewels in some backyards, until he realized they must be swimming pools. They got smaller and smaller. Finally he couldn't make them out at all. The plane levelled off, and everything got quiet.

Maybe this is what I'll do for the rest of my life, he thought as they cruised among the clouds. *Fly!*

Now, through breaks in the clouds, he could see the mountain peaks. Some still had snow on them.

Far below, he could see moving specks. Birds! He was flying above the birds!

No wonder Grandpa Rumpel is always talking about his flying days!

The plane droned on. The afghan lady fell asleep. Other people were reading or talking. The man in the seat in front of him was looking out the window through binoculars.

Then Morris discovered the aircraft safety manual in the pocket of the seat ahead. He was delighted to find it had all kinds of information about the plane — how to put on your life jacket, where the emergency exits were and, best of all, how to use your oxygen mask. *Totally excellent!* thought Morris. *I wonder if it's free?*

The more he thought about it, the more he wanted the manual. But what if he wasn't supposed to take it? He glanced carefully around. Beside him, the afghan lady was dozing, her knitting in a heap on her lap.

With one quick movement, Morris slipped the manual between the pages of Leah's horse magazine. Then, turning his face to the window, he pretended to study the clouds.

Suddenly he heard a voice. "Come with me, Morris. The captain would like to talk to you!"

Morris jumped. Looking up, he saw the beautiful stewardess. She was standing in the aisle, wiggling her finger at him.

"Me?" he croaked. She nodded.

Had she seen him hiding the aircraft manual? What was going to happen to him now? What would his grandparents say if they heard about this? Worse, what would his parents say?

"I don't . . . uh . . . think I can get out," mumbled Morris.

"Of course you can, dear!" said the afghan lady. Now fully awake, she rose ponderously and stood in the aisle.

The stewardess was smiling her dazzling smile. The other passengers were smiling. *Nobody knows,* thought Morris. *Nobody knows I'm ripping off the airline!*

There was only one thing to do. As he sidled out, he slid Leah's magazine with its incriminating evidence deep into the seat pocket. Then, breathing a sigh of relief, he followed the stewardess to the front of the plane.

As he stepped into the cockpit, the pilot and co-pilot turned and smiled at him. Morris grinned back.

"Oh, boy!" he said. "What a beautiful instrument panel! Look! There's something up in the corner of your weather radar screen."

"That's right, son. There's a thunderstorm disturbance off to the left. But it's too far away to bother us on this flight. I see you know something about planes."

Morris blushed. "Sometimes I read Grandpa Rumpel's flying magazines. He used to be a Spitfire pilot. I might be a pilot, too, some day, because I've probably got some of his genes."

"Well, good luck, boy. Enjoy the rest of the flight!"

"I sure will!"

Smiling proudly, Morris returned to his seat. "Well," said the afghan lady. "How did you like the cockpit?"

"It was awesome! My Grandpa Rumpel is a pilot, too, you know."

"Does he still fly?"

"Not anymore. He and Grandma have a ranch beside Cranberry Lake, and I'm going there for a holiday. It'll be cool, because they've got all kinds of wild animals around there!"

"Like moose and bear, I suppose."

"Well, more like deer and stuff. And hawks. Grandpa says this year they've got some very special hawks nesting near Rumpel Ranch. But it's kind of a secret."

It was then that Morris became aware of the man in the seat ahead of him. Even though it was warm in the plane, he was wearing a black leather coat. As they flew, he scanned the mountainside with his binoculars. Then, as Morris chattered on, he suddenly turned his head, as if to listen.

But at that moment the flight attendants began serving trays of food, and Morris forgot about everything else. "Let the good times roll!" he cried, eagerly opening his first little plastic container.

It held a small chicken salad and a big pickle. There was also a bun and a piece of carrot cake, and a Coke. Morris quickly ate it all. Luckily, the afghan lady wasn't hungry, so he ate hers as well.

"How did you enjoy your light snack?" asked the stewardess when she came to collect the trays.

"It certainly was light," said Morris.

6

A short time later, the plane taxied to a stop in front of the Cranberry Corners terminal. The passengers who were leaving gathered their things together and struggled out into the aisle.

Morris squeezed past the afghan lady. "Goodbye," he said. "Thanks for your lunch!"

Suddenly the man in the black leather coat stood up and elbowed his way into the aisle behind Morris. *He must be a bird-watcher or something,* thought Morris. *He's wearing two pairs of binoculars.*

As they shuffled towards the door, he heard the stewardess say, "Are you sure you want to get off here, sir? Your ticket takes you all the way to Port George."

"I have changed my mind," the man snapped. "It is my wish to deplane here — in Cranberry!"

Morris turned around. "Cranberry Corners," he said helpfully.

The man inspected him coldly. "Whatever," he shrugged.

Morris felt a little prickle run down his spine. *He's got icicle eyes,* he thought. *Hard and sharp, like pale-blue icicles!*

As Morris filed off the plane, the stewardess smiled her dazzling smile at him. "Come and fly with us again," she said.

"I sure will!" replied Morris. Then he winked. It was the best wink he'd ever done.

As he trudged across the tarmac, he heard behind him the clickety footsteps of the man in the black leather coat. Lugging his backpack and clutching his nasturtiums, Morris hurried towards the small wooden building marked CRANBERRY CORNERS TERMINAL.

As he got near, he saw two people waving through the window at him, and in a moment he was engulfed in his grandparents' woolly embrace.

They both had on Cowichan Indian sweaters and matching tams. They both wore red plaid pants. In fact, thought Morris, if one hadn't been tall and one short, it might be difficult to tell which was which.

At last his grandmother said, "Let me look at you!" Standing back, she gazed up at him.

"My, how you've grown!" Morris was surprised to see how short she had become since he saw her last. Even his grandfather seemed a little shorter.

They were both full of questions. "How is everyone at home . . . how did you like the plane trip . . . have you had lunch . . . are you hungry?"

Morris handed his grandmother the wilted bouquet of nasturtiums. "I went into the cockpit on the plane. Man, you should have seen it, Gramps! It would blow your mind! . . . I am kind of hungry. . . . Have you still got the red pickup?"

"I guess we'll always have that old pickup," laughed his grandfather. "But we don't bring it into town much anymore. Wait until you see our new car!"

"First we'd better get you something to eat," said Grandma. "You're growing like a weed, but you look thin. Don't trip over your shoelaces, dear."

Taking Morris by the arm, she propelled him towards the coffee shop, where he obligingly downed a cheeseburger and chips, chocolate milkshake, and a piece of apple pie slathered in ice cream. As he was slurping up the last of the milkshake, he heard a familiar voice behind him.

"I wish to buy a map of the Cranberry Corner. And I wish it to show the Cranberry Lake."

I know who that is! thought Morris, glancing over his shoulder. For an instant, his eyes locked with the icicle eyes of the man in the black leather coat. Then the man turned away abruptly. Thrusting some money at the cashier and quickly pocketing the change, he elbowed his way out past the other customers.

As his grandfather ushered him grandly into his new-to-them little red sports car, Morris said, "This is great! I sure like visiting you guys. I never get to ride in the front seat back home!"

"Well," said Grandma, sitting squished sideways in the back with her knees up under her chin, "it isn't every day that our big grandson comes to visit! Erasmus, please don't drive so fast. You're not flying an airplane now, you know."

"It just seems fast because you're in the back seat," grumbled Grandpa, easing his foot off the gas.

Eventually they came to a wooden sign announcing RUMPEL RANCH, and they turned off onto a narrow dirt road. Sideswiping trees, they dipped up and down gullies and swerved around bends. At last they came to a rambling log house surrounded by pots of stunted geraniums.

"Nice . . . er . . . flowers," said Morris, getting out of the car.

"They *were*," said Grandma grimly as she struggled out of the back seat.

"Don't talk about it," Grandpa whispered to Morris. "I forgot to close the pasture gate and Fireweed ate 'em."

"Do you think Fireweed will let me ride her this time?"

"Maybe. Later. First, there's something we must do, you and I. I'll tell you all about it tomorrow."

"Poor Morris," said Grandma. "I'm afraid this visit may not be what you expect!"

What's going on? wondered Morris. *Don't they know this is supposed to be my holiday?*

7

"Hey! Here's Rocket!" cried Morris, as a big black dog rushed towards them, tail wagging ferociously.

"He's not much of a watchdog," said Grandma, "but he's still a sweetie." She pushed open the front door, and Morris followed his grandparents into the house.

He was relieved to see that everything looked the same. A large picture of a Spitfire flying through clouds still hung over the chesterfield, while a real wooden propeller with a clock in the middle rested precariously on the fireplace mantel, exactly as it had the year before. On top of the piano stood framed school pictures of Morris, Leah, Quincy and their cousin, Gwen—going back to grade one.

Beside them was an old photo of Grandpa in his air force uniform. Grandma's model horse collection was displayed on window sills and little tables all over the room.

"Well, now," said Grandpa as Morris plopped his backpack onto the kitchen table

41

and began to rummage through it. "Tell me all about your visit to the cockpit of the airplane."

"It was awesome! I saw a thunderstorm on the weather screen!"

"That's great! What was the captain doing?"

"Drinking coffee. The co-pilot was flying. And he was doing a real smooth job of it, too!" Morris dumped everything out of his backpack onto the table. "Mom sent you a plum pudding for having me. It's in here somewhere. You should have seen that instrument panel, Gramps!"

"Pretty impressive, eh?"

"Boy, I'll say! But I'll bet you could fly that plane, Gramps!"

His grandfather's blue eyes sparkled. "Wouldn't I like to!" Then he pointed to a piece of red cellophane. "Maybe that's my pudding, under that pink thing."

"Yeah, that's it." Morris hauled it out and gave it to him.

Grandpa held the tin, gazing at it lovingly. "One of my favourite foods! We'll have it tonight."

"No, we won't," said Grandma. "Have you forgotten what the doctor said, Erasmus?"

"What did he say?" asked Morris, all ears.

His grandmother's mouth went tight. "Just

that he's seen too many people dig their own graves with a spoon!"

"Ha-ha," Morris giggled nervously. He looked from one to the other, waiting for his grandparents to laugh, too. But they both just looked glum.

"So, uh . . . what's this special thing we're going to do, Gramps?" he asked cheerfully.

"It will have to keep until tomorrow. Right now I promised your grandmother we'd go and get a load of firewood for her. Did you bring some boots? It might be muddy."

"Yeah, they're in here somewhere, I guess." Morris poked through his clothes half-heartedly. "I was wondering about this special thing that you need help with, Gramps. Does it have something to do with looking for that old goldmine you said might be around here?"

"No. Nothing to do with that. Now put your boots on, and we'll go and catch Fireweed. She won't be too happy having to go to work, I'm afraid."

Pulling his boots out from under his clothes, Morris put them on.

"This boy thinks of everything," said Grandma, smiling proudly. "Most his age would have their packs full of comic books!" Morris blushed modestly.

After a drink of milk and two pieces of chocolate cake, Morris was ready. He followed his grandfather to the barn to get the halter and rope, and then they set out to catch Fireweed.

As they opened the gate to the pasture, the big dapple grey horse lifted her head and looked at them. But as soon as she saw the halter, she snorted and walked away, her tail switching.

"Rats!" said Grandpa. "I forgot to hide the darn halter!"

Holding it behind his back, he stalked towards the horse again, followed closely by Morris.

When he got near enough, he made a grab for her mane. Clutching it in one hand, he slipped the halter over her head. "Gotcha!" shouted Grandpa. But before he could get it fastened, Fireweed jerked her head out and took off.

"I'll catch her for you, Gramps!" cried Morris. Picking up the halter, he went leaping across the stubbly field after her. At the other side of the pasture, Fireweed paused to crop some grass.

Hiding the halter behind his back as his grandfather had done, Morris crept forward.

44

Fireweed eyed him suspiciously, but she kept on eating. When he got next to her, he whipped the halter out from behind his back and slipped it on.

Fireweed jerked up her head and sent Morris head over heels backwards. Then she went back to cropping grass.

By now Grandpa Rumpel had arrived. And this time Fireweed graciously allowed herself to be led away.

"I don't think she wants to haul wood today," said Morris as they walked back to the barn.

"Give me a tractor any day," muttered his grandfather. "I almost got one once, you know, but your grandmother wanted this horse so bad . . ."

As he harnessed Fireweed to the wagon, Morris stood stroking her neck. "She's a pretty nice horse, though," he said. "Maybe some day you'll get a tractor, too!"

"It doesn't really matter anymore," said his grandfather. "I'm past caring about them now."

Morris was shocked.

Grandpa past caring about tractors. Suddenly he remembered the plum pudding and what the doctor had said. And now this!

He studied his grandfather closely. He

looked the same as he always had. But then, so had little Hammy, the Rumpels' hamster, the day before they found him huddled at the bottom of his little wheel — dead!

8

Morris sat beside his grandfather, his hands gripping the wooden seat as the old wagon creaked across the field. Directly in front of them and surprisingly close was Fireweed's muscular rump. Her long grey tail switched from side to side, flicking off flies.

As they ambled along in the warm summer sunshine, Morris studied his grandfather. His old peaked cap was tilted over one eye, and he was humming. Whatever he might have wrong with him — if there was something — didn't seem to be bothering him now. Gradually Morris began to relax.

Then, above the cloppity-clop of Fireweed's hooves, he heard a new sound — an eerie, distant sort of wailing.

"What's that, Gramps?"

His grandfather stopped humming and pulled in the reins. In the stillness they listened, and Morris heard it again.

"It's the falcons," said his grandfather. "They're nesting on the cliff by the lake."

47

"Real falcons? Like the ones people used to use for hunting?"

Grandpa nodded. "Still do. Peregrines. Very rare." He clucked to Fireweed, and the big grey horse began to plod on again. "In some parts of the world, people pay thousands of dollars for them."

Morris's head reeled. "Wow! Thousands?"

"Of course, it's illegal to take them from the wild."

"But what if they're on our own property, like these?"

"Not even then. They're protected by law."

"But maybe we could let people come and look at them! Quincy and Leah and me could sell tickets. We could set up little benches and sell lemonade and—"

"No way!" interrupted Grandpa. "We wouldn't want anything to disturb their nesting. And we especially don't want any poachers finding out about them. Right now, only you and I and Grandma know about these birds, and that's the way we want to keep it. The falcons are safer that way."

"Now I remember! I've seen them in pictures. They had little leather leashes on their legs. I wonder if any other birds ever have to wear leashes?"

"I sincerely hope not."

When they got to the woodlot, Fireweed was given hay to eat, while Morris and his grandfather piled wood in the wagon.

After a while, Grandpa sat down abruptly on a log. "There, that's enough. Time for a rest now." He wiped his forehead with a big red handkerchief.

"Are you all right?" Morris looked at him worriedly.

"Just hot." Reaching into his pocket, Grandpa took out two limp-looking chocolate bars. "Don't tell your grandmother!" he said with a wink, giving one to Morris.

As they sat there eating their snack, they suddenly heard a rapid fluttering of wings overhead.

Grandpa squinted up into the treetops. "I think it's one of the falcons," he whispered. "Look!"

Craning his neck, Morris caught a flash of something dark-grey and white . . . and then it was gone. "Gee, I guess I just saw about five hundred dollars' worth," he said.

"You saw something very special. There aren't many breeding pairs of Peale's peregrine falcons around—only about sixty on the Queen

Charlotte Islands, and that's the largest population of them in the world."

"Gee!" said Morris, licking the last of the melted chocolate from his wrapper.

"Well, time to go," said Grandpa, and they climbed back into the wagon.

"Can I drive?" asked Morris.

"Are you sure you can handle it?" asked his grandfather. "When Fireweed smells the barn, she puts on the power, you know."

"No problem, Gramps."

So Grandpa handed him the reins, and they rumbled off.

All went well until they came around the last bend, and Fireweed decided to speed things up. As she spurted for home, Morris clung to the reins for dear life. He was sure he was going to bounce right off the seat.

"How-ow-ow do I s-s-stop her?" he cried.

"Don't worry," said Grandpa. "She'll stop."

They rattled and bumped right up to the barn door, when Fireweed suddenly stopped in her tracks.

"That's it," said Grandpa. "That's as far as she goes."

"Man!" said Morris, handing back the reins and rubbing his red hands. "I never thought she could go so fast. That sure gave me an appetite! I hope Grandma's got supper ready."

"Not so fast, there," said Grandpa Rumpel. "First we have to look after our horse. Here, you can put this in the barn for me." And he began taking off the leather harness.

As Morris lugged it into the barn, he felt something bunt him from behind. Turning around, he found himself gazing up into Fireweed's long grey face.

"You'd better go faster than that!" laughed Grandpa. Harness jangling, Morris scurried into the barn with Fireweed snorting behind him.

While his grandfather put hay and oats in the horse's stall, Morris filled the water bucket.

Finally Grandpa said, "There! Now let's go and see about supper."

It's about time! thought Morris, wiping his sweaty forehead.

After three helpings of chicken and dumplings, he began to feel better. And when his grandmother brought him a large dish of fresh raspberries topped with ice cream, he felt quite restored.

"Where's my ice cream?" grunted Grandpa, looking in disgust at his bowl of plain berries.

"You don't need any," said Grandma.

Squishing his berries into his ice cream to make it pink, Morris asked, "Does your special project have something to do with the falcons, Gramps?"

Picking at his raspberries, his grandfather shook his head.

What could it be? By now Morris was consumed with curiosity. "It's a boat, isn't it?" he blurted out. "You're going to build a boat and you want me to help!"

"Not a boat. Don't worry. You'll find out soon enough. Right now I'm going to watch the news."

His grandparents moved into the livingroom, turned on the TV, settled in their easy chairs and promptly fell asleep.

Morris, happily full and recovered from his exhausting day, went outside.

Rocket was lying on the porch, sleeping.

"Want to chase some sticks, Rocket?"

But the old black dog just opened one eye briefly, then closed it again and went back to sleep.

Morris wandered over to the barn. It was cool and dark and quiet inside. The only sound was Fireweed chomping hay in her stall.

Behind the barn, almost lost in the shadows

of the trees, was an old shed — Grandpa's work-shop. *I wonder if the special project is in there,* thought Morris. *It wouldn't hurt to have a look.*

It was fast getting dark, and the dew had fallen. As he scuffed through the wet grass, his eyes were on the shed. *There's something funny about the roof,* he thought. *Like a bump, where there shouldn't be a bump . . .*

Then he saw the pale, ghostly face. Two eyes peered down at him. For a moment Morris stood frozen in his tracks.

It's just an owl, he told himself. *I've seen owls before.*

Still, it was spooky. So spooky that he almost turned around and ran. But he was so close now, and so curious to see what was in the shed . . .

He couldn't quite reach the window, so he dragged over a chunk of wood and stood on it. Clinging to the window sill, he peered in. The shed was dim and silent. As his eyes grew accustomed to the darkness inside, he was able to make out his grandfather's workbench, and on it, a long wooden box.

Morris felt a shiver run down his spine.

A coffin! The special project was a coffin!!!!

9

Suddenly Morris heard a ghostly *Hooo, hooo* above him. There was a rustle of wings, and the owl swooped off the roof and vanished into the trees. Morris leaped from his perch. Slipping and skidding, he tore past the barn, straight for the lights of the house.

He burst into the kitchen, shutting the door tight behind him. Right away his nose began to twitch. For the moment forgetting about the workshop and his grisly discovery, Morris cried, "What do I smell?"

"Bread!" said his grandmother as she took some pans from the oven. Tapping them briskly on their bottoms, she tipped the steaming loaves out onto a rack. "There! Two for the Cranberry Suzies' bake sale, and two for us." She smiled at Morris. "Where have you been? Out exploring?"

I wonder if she knows about the coffin! "Sort of," he answered warily.

"I'll cut us some nice fresh bread as soon as

it cools," said his grandmother. Then, to Morris's horror, she burst into tears!

Rushing over to him, she hugged him tight. "Oh, Morris! I'm so glad you're here!"

She knows! he thought, gasping for breath. *She knows what's in the workshop!*

Reaching up, he patted her shoulder awkwardly. "Don't worry, Grandma," he said. "Grandpa still looks pretty healthy."

"I know," she sniffled. "But it's just so wonderful to have a hungry boy in the house again!" Blinking back her tears, she let go of Morris. "I know your grandfather looks just fine," she continued. "But he's got his mind made up that he's going to take off some time this summer, and nothing is going to stop him. He and his Wings of Icarus!"

Morris looked puzzled. "What's that?"

"That's what he calls his special project. His 'Wings of Icarus.'"

"Wow! Do Mom and Dad know about all this stuff?"

"No. Your grandfather wants to surprise them. He figures he'll be about ready when they come to pick you up. He says he wants everybody to be here when he soars off into the wild blue yonder."

This is really heavy! thought Morris. "Where's Grandpa now?" he asked, looking around. "Is he finished watching the news?"

"It's all over. He's probably in the bathroom studying his celestial navigation. Do you want to watch some TV with me? There's a special on the return of the buff-bellied hummingbird."

How can she be like this? Doesn't she care about Grandpa at all? "Um, no, thanks. I'm kind of tired. I think I'll just go to bed."

"Of course. I understand." And she kissed him goodnight. "You've had a long day. Don't forget to clean your teeth."

"You sound just like Mom!"

But by the time his grandfather came out of the bathroom, Morris was sound asleep.

10

Morris didn't know if it was a dream or real. But he woke suddenly, thinking he had heard a car down below in the driveway.

The house was silent. Pale moonlight filtered in through the window. Morris lay wide-eyed in his four-poster bed, staring at the foot of his bed. *Is that someone standing there? Maybe — the man in the black leather coat?!*

Morris huddled under the covers, grateful for the comforting weight of Rocket lying across his feet.

The shape at the foot of the bed didn't move. Finally summoning all his courage, Morris reached over and turned on his light.

There, draped over the bedpost, were his clothes. He got up and removed them. Then he padded over to the window and looked out.

Moonlight flooded the driveway and yard below. There was no car.

Morris opened his door, and the comforting sounds of gentle snoring came wafting from his grandparents' room. He climbed back into bed, tucked his feet under Rocket, and was soon fast asleep again.

* * *

The next time he woke, the sun was streaming in. Outside, birds were chirping, chickens were cackling, and somebody was singing. Morris listened sleepily.

"Oh, off we go . . . into the wild blue yonder . . . flying high. . . . into the sky . . ." boomed a voice.

All at once, Morris remembered where he was. He got up and looked out the window. Down below, he saw his grandfather striding through a flock of chickens towards the barn.

Just then, two shadows passed overhead, one behind the other. Morris leaned out, craning his neck. "It's the falcons!" he cried, as two magnificent hawks swooped by. Looking up, he could see their white breasts and the undersides of their great barred wings.

They flew over the barn and disappeared somewhere in the fields beyond.

Morris scrambled into his clothes, sprinkled his face with water and ran downstairs, leaving his bed to Rocket.

His grandmother was in the kitchen. "I just

saw the falcons!" Morris told her. "They flew right over the top of my head!"

"Aren't they beautiful?" said Grandma. "I call them Charles and Diana, because they're so regal-looking. Now, let me make you some porridge. It will only take me a jiffy in the new micro!"

"But I don't like . . ." began Morris, but his grandmother was already measuring things into a bowl. Placing it carefully in the microwave oven, she began pushing buttons.

"I think you pushed too many buttons," Morris told her, peering at the rubbery blob that emerged several minutes later. Grandma agreed, so he happily filled up on two bowls of Krispy Krunchies and five pieces of toast.

"I wonder which one is Charles and which one is Diana?" he mused, pouring himself some more orange juice.

"Diana's probably the big one. Usually the girl falcons are."

"Yeah, like spiders. Do you suppose their eggs are hatched yet?"

"I'm sure they are. That's why we don't want anyone to find out about the nest. The fledglings could be easily taken by poachers right now."

"What would happen to them?"

"They'd be sold for breeding stock or falconry. Maybe end up in a bazaar in Baghdad or some place, poor things! By the way, Grandpa said to tell you he'd be waiting for you in the workshop. He says there's no time to waste."

No time to waste! The words rang ominously in Morris's head as he slowly set out for his grandfather's workshop.

11

There's nothing spooky about the workshop in the daylight, thought Morris, as he approached the old building. Birds sang in the trees overhead, sunshine flooded the building with light, and there were no owls on the roof.

He peered in the open door. His grandfather's back was towards him. He was standing beside the workbench, gazing into the long wooden box.

Oh, man! This is too heavy for me! thought Morris. *What will I say to him? "That's a skookum coffin, Grandpa!?"*

Finally he blurted out, "YO!"

"Oh, good morning, Morris!" said Grandpa Rumpel, turning around.

Keeping his eyes resolutely off the workbench, Morris stalled for time. "Charles and Diana just flew over the barn! Did you see them?"

"Yes. They're probably out hunting. Well, come on in, boy. Don't just stand there! There's work to be done!"

Morris shuffled forward.

"Behold!" said Grandpa. "In this simple box lies the means by which I will shortly take off from this poor earth, to soar like Charles and Diana, into the very heavens!"

Gathering up his courage, Morris peered into the box. He didn't know what he was expecting to see, but it was certainly not some bright-red shiny cloth! Quincy had once told him a ghost story about shrouds. Could this be one?

"What do you think?" asked Grandpa. "Bright enough?"

Morris gulped. "It's nice and cheery. Is it a . . . a . . . a sort of do-it-yourself kit?"

"That's right. And you're going to help me! I thought red would be nice and noticeable when I'm up there flying around. You'll be able to see me for miles!"

Lifting out the red cloth, Grandpa laid it to one side. Then he took out some aluminum poles.

"Now, let's get busy on my Wings of Icarus! This old pilot is going to fly again!"

"Oh, wow! It's a hang-glider kit!" Morris was so relieved that he nearly fainted on the spot.

"And there's my harness!" His grandfather

pointed to some straps and buckles hanging on the wall.

"Way to go, Gramps! Can I do it, too? Quincy would go nuts if she saw me flying!"

His grandfather shook his head. "No way! Not until you're older. But you can learn a lot by helping me with this one. Well, let's get going. I want to get it finished and get practised up before your folks come to collect you. I can't wait to see their faces when they see me airborne!" Rubbing his hands together, Grandpa chortled gleefully.

Together they set the box on the floor. Then, using Grandpa's new tool set, they began fitting pieces of tubing together.

They worked all morning, all afternoon and after supper, until Grandpa said, "I think we've done enough for one day. Let's go in and watch some television."

"Right on!" said Morris. "Can I pop some popcorn?"

"Admirable idea!"

Just as they got settled comfortably in the living-room—Grandpa Rumpel in his swivel rocker, and Morris stretched out on the chesterfield with a bowl of popcorn on his stomach—Grandma came in.

"Did you remember to lock up the chickens?" she asked.

"Well, dag nab it!" said Grandpa. "We forgot all about those dumb chickens! Morris, how would you like to be a good scout and do it?"

"They have to be locked up or the raccoons will get them," Grandma told Morris. "I'll turn on the porch light for you."

Stuffing another handful of popcorn into his mouth, Morris struggled to his feet. Outside in the shadowy backyard, he was grateful for the light from the porch.

In the chicken-house, the hens were on their roost for the night. Some were still squawking as they pushed and shoved each other along. *They don't seem to like each other too much,* thought Morris. *But I guess they feel safe all squished together like that.*

He closed the rough wooden door and fastened it with the bolt. But just as he turned to go, he heard a faint rustle in the blackberry bushes behind him. Something was moving!

Morris turned to look, and the rustling stopped. For a few seconds he stood transfixed, staring. *There's something in there,* he thought. *Something . . . or somebody!*

He raced for the house. When he reached it,

he slammed the door shut behind him and locked it.

Someone was singing in the living-room. Morris rushed in to find his grandmother seated at the piano. She was picking out notes with one finger, and singing.

"There's a . . . there's a . . . there's . . ." stammered Morris breathlessly.

His grandfather held his finger up to his lips. "Ssssh! She's practising."

"But I saw a—"

"The Cranberry Suzies are doing 'The Sound of Music,' and your grandma's one of the nuns," whispered Grandpa.

At last Grandma reached the end of her song. She smiled at Morris. "Did you get the chickens locked up?"

"Yes, but there's somebody out there! I saw somebody in the bushes! With a mask!"

"Sounds like a raccoon," grunted Grandpa, turning the TV back on.

"That must have been what you saw, dear," said Grandma. "There's a family of them around this year."

"It sure looked like a face!" said Morris, settling himself once again on the chesterfield with his popcorn. He was not completely convinced.

Suddenly he sat bolt upright, sending popcorn flying in all directions. "Now somebody's looking in the window!"

Grandpa turned off the television.

"Maybe it's a poacher!" Morris whispered hoarsely.

Everyone stared at the window. A long, pale, mournful face stared back.

Grandpa began to laugh. "It's just Fireweed!"

"Oh, that poor horse," cried Grandma. "She's trying to tell us she wants her supper."

"Well, don't listen to her." Grandpa put on his boots. "She's had her supper. We just didn't close the barn door. You stay here this time, Morris. I'll put her away."

Morris was only too happy to stay. "Do you think Fireweed was really trying to tell us something?" he asked his grandmother. "Like, maybe warn us?"

"I don't think she's that smart," said Grandma.

But Morris wasn't so sure.

12

A few days later, Morris was sitting on a stool in the workshop, handing tools to his grandfather.

"I sure hope poachers don't find Charles and Diana's nest! Did you know their babies might end up in a Baghdad bazaar, Gramps?"

"So your grandma tells me. I know that falconry is still very popular in that part of the world. . . . Hand me those small pliers, please."

"And did you know that falcons won't hunt unless they're really hungry? That means their owners don't feed them if they want them to catch birds. I think that's a maxi-bummer, man!"

"Sounds as if you've been reading Grandma's bird books."

"Yeah. I was looking at one this morning. There was a picture of a peregrine falcon with a hood on its head. It had a leash around its foot that was attached to a post. I'll bet Charles and Diana would hate that!"

"Some people call it sport, Morris. Here, let's get this wing fitted on."

"It's going to be finished pretty soon, isn't it? I sure wish I could try hang-gliding."

"Maybe when you're older. It will be something for you to look forward to."

"There's a whole bunch of things I'm supposed to be looking forward to. I need something I can do right now. How about letting me ride Fireweed?"

"We'll think about it," said Grandpa. "Your grandma rode her a few times, until she slid off into Fireweed's bathtub of drinking water one day. Said Fireweed was just too slippery without a saddle."

"I wouldn't need a saddle!"

"Well, I suppose if the ancient Greeks rode bareback, you can, too. Remind me, and I'll give you a practice session after lunch."

As soon as lunch was over, Grandpa was reminded of his promise, and Morris prepared for his first riding lesson.

First, his grandfather changed Fireweed's halter for a bit and bridle with leather reins.

"Does she like that thing in her mouth?" wondered Morris.

"It's just a snaffle bit. They're gentle. You

have to have something to control a big horse like this."

As he stood beside Fireweed's towering flank, Morris began to get qualms. "How do I get on?"

"That's the easy part. Just don't forget Rule Number One. Always mount from a horse's left side. Don't ask me why. Now, come here and I'll give you a leg-up."

Putting one foot on his grandfather's cupped hands, Morris heaved himself onto the horse's broad back. Clutching the reins in both hands, he looked down at the chickens running around below, and at the top of his grandfather's head.

"Hey, no sweat! I like riding!" he said, grinning broadly.

"You haven't gone anywhere yet. Now, grip with your knees. And don't yank on the reins!"

Just then Grandma came tearing out of the house waving something. "Don't let him ride without head protection!" she cried. "That horse is slippery!"

"Oh, Grandma! I don't need it! I'm not going to fall off!" said Morris as she thrust a white bicycle helmet up at him.

"Wear it! And do up the chin strap!"

After a slight argument about who should

lead horse and rider around the paddock, Grandma took hold of the reins, and they set off.

"Why can't I hold my own reins?" grumbled Morris. "I feel like a little kid!"

"You can eventually. First Fireweed has to get used to you. She's really a work horse, you know. She's not used to having anyone on her back. Some day when I get a saddle, I'll ride her more. Are you getting the feel of it?"

"Sure! This is easy! Can I go by myself?"

His grandmother looked doubtful. "Let the boy go," said Grandpa.

"All right," said Grandma. "But hang on, Morris, and don't yank the reins!"

Fireweed walked sedately around the paddock. "I'm doing it! I'm doing it!" cried Morris. "I might be a jockey when I grow up!"

"Well, at least you stayed on," said his grandfather, helping Morris dismount after several circuits of the paddock. "And that's something. Even the ancient Greeks had to start from there."

* * *

Morris, who was getting a little bored handing tools to his grandfather, could hardly wait for

70

the next day and his second riding lesson. As soon as lunch was over, he asked, "Can I try galloping today?"

Grandpa shook his head. "I don't want to stop work on the hang-glider right now." And he rushed back out to his workshop.

"Grandma? Will you put the bit and stuff on Fireweed, so I can try galloping?"

But his grandmother was dressed in her nun's outfit, and was already getting out her car keys. "Oh, I'm sorry, Morris. But I'm late for rehearsal. Anyway, you shouldn't even be thinking about galloping yet." And she bustled out the front door to the little red sports car, her long black skirt flapping around her ankles.

I don't really need any more lessons, thought Morris. *I can do it myself.* Putting on his bicycle helmet, he went out to look for Fireweed.

Luckily, she was already in the paddock with her halter on. Morris wasn't too sure about the bit and bridle, so he decided just to snap the reins to her halter.

"Here I come, Fireweed. Now, just hold still, there's a good horse.... Ooops! Sorry, dropped it. Here we go again. Please lift up your head, Fireweed. Please!"

At last he managed to get the reins attached.

Taking hold of them, he led her over to the fence. He tied the reins loosely to it, then climbed up on the rails.

Fireweed lowered her head to eat some grass, and Morris was able to wiggle onto her back. At last he sat up. "I'm on!" he cried.

But he had forgotten about the reins. They were still tied to the fence.

Suddenly Fireweed snorted and tossed her head. The reins jerked loose, and she took off.

"Help!" hollered Morris, clutching her mane and hanging on for dear life.

Head high and tail flying, Fireweed trotted around and around the paddock. To Morris, everything was a blur as they flew past.

At last the terrible ride came to an end. Fireweed suddenly skidded to a stop. Giving a snort, she lowered her head and began to drink from her bathtub as Morris toppled into it.

Fireweed looked down at her rider. Then she dribbled a mouthful of water onto him.

"You're just a mean old horse!" spluttered Morris, climbing out of the tub.

He squished his soggy way into the house and changed his clothes. After a snack in the kitchen to restore his strength, he went over to the workshop. He found his grandfather rechecking his fittings.

"There," he said. "Almost finished! Maybe we'll have time for a riding lesson before supper."

"Uh, that's okay," said Morris. "I don't think I feel like one just now."

* * *

A few days later, Grandpa announced, "Well, tomorrow's the big day! The Wings of Icarus are finished!" Putting away his tools, he inspected his handiwork lovingly.

"Are you sure you know how to fly it?" asked Morris. "Sometimes it's better to take these things . . . er . . . slowly."

"Nah. I was born to fly. Piece of cake! It's like riding a bicycle. You just lean this way and that. Nothing to it, for an old pilot like me."

And so the launch was set for the next day. "The wind starts blowing onshore at approximately 08:00 hours. I shall take off at exactly 09:00," said Grandpa.

The next morning, everybody was up early. Grandma was getting ready for the Cranberry Suzies' bake sale, and Morris and Grandpa were preparing for the launch.

Wearing new striped overalls and an old leather flying helmet, Grandpa looked anxiously out the window. Clouds were gathering over Cranberry Lake. "It does not look good," he groaned.

"The TV says rain and thunderstorms," reported Morris.

Grandpa took off his helmet. "We'll have to scrub the launch for today."

"Oh, good! Then you can both come to the bake sale!" said Grandma. "There will be entertainment, you know. We Suzies are going to sing one of our pieces from the musical. And they're serving strawberries and ice cream."

Morris wiggled his eyebrows at his grandfather. "Let's go, Grandpa! I've got lots of money to spend!"

"Well, I suppose I could get some fabric mender from the hardware store, in case I snag my sails. All right, we'll go."

"And you can both get haircuts while we're in town," added Grandma, looking at Morris's shaggy locks. "You certainly need it."

13

As they got ready to drive into town, Grandma began taking packages out of the freezer. "You can put these in the trunk of the car for me," she said to Morris. "They're cookies and things for the bake sale."

"All these?" cried Morris. "I didn't know you'd been making all this stuff!"

"Neither did I," said Grandpa.

"I didn't intend you two to know," said Grandma.

When they got to the community hall in Cranberry Corners, the door had just opened. "Wow!" said Morris. "Look at all the people!"

"It looks as if all of Cranberry Corners will be going on a diet next week," observed his grandfather.

"Some of them might be coming for the entertainment, you know," said Grandma. "After all, the Suzies are quite famous. And there's also the white elephant booth."

"What's that?" wondered Morris.

"It's where they sell all kinds of things," said

his grandmother. "Collectibles, and odds and ends."

"Junk," said Grandpa.

Clutching his money, Morris cruised the big hall. As in a dream, he drifted past tables loaded with cookies, squares, pies and cakes. One table had nothing but chocolate cakes!

He circled the room a second time. At last he homed in on the pies. There were apple pies, their crusts sprinkled with sugar; blackberry pies with dark-red juice oozing out of their tops; and quivering lemon pies covered with golden meringue.

"How much are they?" he asked.

"Five dollars," said the Suzie in charge.

Morris gulped. "Each?"

"Yes. Would you like one?"

Nodding, Morris took his money out of his wallet and counted it.

"We have apple, blackberry or lemon."

"I know," said Morris. Then, his face flushed, he suddenly handed over three five-dollar bills. "One of each, please!"

The Suzie put his pies in boxes for him. Cradling them in his arms, he backed carefully away from the table.

Morris struggled through the crowd looking

for his grandfather. He finally found him buying butter tarts.

"Look what I got, Gramps! Pies!"

"Good show!" said Grandpa Rumpel. "Let's take this stuff to the car."

On their way to the door, Morris spotted the white elephant booth.

"Could I just take a look, Gramps?"

"Sure. I'll hold your pies. But don't spend all your money."

"I almost already did. I just have forty-five cents left."

Grandpa Rumpel waited by the door, and in a few minutes Morris appeared out of the crowd.

"Boy, I sure like white elephants," he said. "Look what I got for forty-five cents. A bird book! See, it's got all kinds of birds in it. Even falcons! And it's not even worn out!"

"Well, I'll be darned! Now that's what I call a good buy!"

For the next little while, they sat in the car eating butter tarts and looking at Morris's bird book. Outside the rain was still drizzling down, but they didn't care.

"This has sure been my lucky day," said Morris. "Wait until I show this to Quincy! Let's see what it says about Charles and Diana." He leafed through the book until he came to the section on hawks. "Listen to this, Gramps! It says that for its size the peregrine falcon is probably the most powerful bird of prey that flies. And its courage is as great as its power! Did you know it's capable of speeds of up to a hundred miles an hour? What's that in kilometres, Gramps?"

"About a hundred and sixty k.p.h., I guess. That's as fast as a small training plane," marvelled Grandpa Rumpel.

"Wow!"

"Well, that's the last of the butter tarts," said Grandpa, brushing crumbs off his chest. "I suppose we'd better be getting to the hardware store."

"What about our strawberries and ice cream?"

"We'll come back later for those."

They hurried along the street in the rain and wind, ducking gratefully inside the hardware store when they came to it.

While his grandfather looked for fabric mender, Morris wandered around. He inspected fishing poles and tool boxes and baseballs and bicycles, and wished he hadn't spent all his money on pies.

It was then that he heard an impatient voice on the other side of a stack of garden hoses.

"But I just wish to buy a gunny sack! Is there not any place in Cranberry Corner where I can obtain a plain gunny sack?"

Morris peeked around the corner. *It's him! It's old Icicle Eyes!*

The man was talking to the clerk. *She's sort of a younger version of the stewardess,* thought Morris. *Maybe she's her sister!* Taking a comb from his hip pocket, he quickly combed his hair.

"I'm afraid I don't know, sir," said the clerk, smiling in a friendly fashion at the man in the black leather coat.

Then Grandpa Rumpel appeared from behind a display of rubber beach balls. "Maybe I can help," he said in his booming voice. "You'll probably find gunny sacks at the feed store on the edge of town."

"Oh, hello, Mr. Rumpel!" said the clerk. "I didn't see you come in!"

At the mention of the name "Rumpel," the man in the leather coat fastened his ice-blue stare on Grandpa. Then, giving a slight, stiff little bow, he turned and marched out the door.

"Let's go and get those strawberries and ice cream now," said Grandpa, spotting Morris peeking out from behind the hoses. "As soon as I pay this young lady."

"Are you sure you're all finished, Gramps?" asked Morris, running the comb through his hair again. "I don't mind hanging around here for a while."

"You've just reminded me. We still have to go to the barber."

When they got outside, Grandpa said, "If Al is too busy, we'll just forget about it. I don't intend to miss our strawberries."

But Al the barber wasn't busy. "Everybody's at the bake sale," he complained. "How would you both like an astronaut special? I've got them on sale this week."

"Sounds good," said Grandpa. "You go first, Morris."

As he snipped and clipped, Al chatted. "You folks expecting company? Had a customer in here the other day asking about Rumpel Ranch."

"Nope. Nobody's been around," answered Grandpa.

"He was a funny sort of guy. Not very friendly. Said he was waiting for a friend to arrive with a boat to go fishing. He heard the fish were biting pretty good around your end of the lake. Has your grandpa taken you out fishing yet?" Al asked Morris, running the clippers up the back of his head.

"No." Morris stared at his reflection in the mirror. *I'm practically bald,* he thought. *I didn't know an astronaut special would look like this!*

When they finally came out of the barber shop an hour later, he said, "My ears feel kind of cold."

"Blame it on your grandmother," said Grandpa.

* * *

They were sitting at a little table eating their strawberries and ice cream when Grandma found them.

"Good grief!" she said. "I didn't know you!"

"We've been to Al's," Morris told her. "He gave us astronaut specials. And he gave me some of my hair to take home."

"I wasn't really thinking of crew cuts," said Grandma. "But I guess I'll get used to you. You missed all the entertainment, you know. We even got to sing an encore."

It wasn't until they were on their way home that Morris thought again about the man in the black leather coat. He was just about to tell his grandparents about him, when he suddenly thought, *What if they get mad at me for talking on the plane about special hawks? And what if old Icicle Eyes is really going to go fishing with his friend? And what's the gunny sack for? Fish?*

But Grandma chattered on about the bake sale all the way home, so Morris said nothing.

* * *

That evening after supper, when his grandparents were out locking up the animals, the phone rang. Morris leaped to answer it.

"Rumpel Ranch!" he announced.

"Morris? Is that you?" asked his mother. "You sound different. Are you all right?"

"Oh, hi, Mom! Sure I'm all right. I'm eating some pie."

"Are you homesick? Do you miss us?"

"Nope. We went to a bake sale today, and you should see the stuff we got! I got a bird book, too. And I've been helping Grandpa with his Wings of Icarus. He's going to take off for the wild blue yonder tomorrow if it isn't raining. But I'm not supposed to tell you about it. It's a secret. Tell Quincy I've been riding Fireweed bareback all over the place! I'm practically an expert!"

"Oh, do be careful!" said his mother. "What kind of wings did you say? Licorice?"

"Icarus," mumbled Morris.

"How about the chores? I hope you're help-ing with the chores."

"I don't think they have any chores here."

"Well, tell Grandma and Grandpa we're coming to pick you up on the weekend."

"Already? Do I have to go home already?"

"It's still a few days away," said his mother. "Don't eat Grandma out of house and home before we get there!"

"Don't worry," said Morris. "I bought a whole bunch of food for them today."

14

When Morris woke up the next morning, he hurried over to the open window. Some time during the night, the weather had cleared. Now only a few fleecy clouds scudded across the blue sky.

"Hooray!" he shouted.

Down in the kitchen, his grandmother was swishing around in her nun's costume. His grandfather was outfitted once again in his striped overalls and flying helmet.

"All systems are 'go' for the launch!" announced Grandpa. "Hurry up and eat breakfast, everybody."

"But I have to go to another rehearsal this morning," said Grandma, wiping marmalade off her long black sleeve. "Besides, I don't think I could bear to watch you in that hang-glider!"

"That's all right. We can manage, can't we, Morris?"

Grandma looked worried. "You're not going to fly over the lake, I hope."

"Don't worry, Grandma," said Morris. "Grandpa was born to fly!"

"Anyway, today I'm just doing a little test flight over the bean field." Taking off his glasses, Grandpa polished them on his serviette. "I'll be landing right behind the barn."

After breakfast, Grandma took off for town. Morris and Grandpa proceeded to the workshop. The hang-glider, checked and rechecked and re-rechecked, stood ready, its glossy red wings folded.

Carrying his harness, Grandpa led off, the folded glider sloping downwards from his shoulder to Morris's.

As they trudged across the field to the cliff beside the lake, Morris scanned the sky. "I wonder if the babies are flying yet? Charles and Diana's, I mean."

"They're probably still in the nest. But I guess it won't be long before they are."

"I hope they do before I go home. I'd love to see them. My bird book says they lay two to four eggs—" Suddenly Morris stopped chattering. "Gramps! I hear an outboard motor!"

They had reached the cliff at the edge of the lake now. Together they looked down and saw a small boat going slowly along the shoreline.

It had a little roof over the front and two men sitting in the back.

"It's just someone fishing," said Grandpa. "See the poles rigged on the rails?"

"I was afraid they were poachers," said Morris as the boat disappeared around a point of land.

"I don't think so. They look pretty innocent. Besides, no one knows about the falcons being here."

Morris felt his face getting red. "Gramps," he began, "I was telling this lady on the plane all about . . ."

But his grandfather was busy licking his finger and holding it up into the wind. "I think this is a dandy place for the launch, Morris. Let's get things ready."

They set the glider down on the grass. Then they unfolded its wings and began to prepare for the flight. By 08:30 hours everything was ready.

"Now we just have to wait for the right wind," said Grandpa. So they sat down on the grass and waited.

"It's sure beautiful with its wings open, isn't it?" Morris stroked the silky cloth.

"Just wait until you see us in the air. For this

86

first time I'll just soar around here a little bit, and then I'll fly over to the bean patch. You can meet me there in about fifteen minutes. Understood?"

"Understood!"

At exactly 09:00 hours, the wind came up off the lake. Grandpa stood up and buckled himself into the hang-glider.

As he stood poised at the edge of the cliff with the Wings of Icarus outstretched above him, Morris thought, *He looks just like an ancient Greek!*

"See you in the bean patch!" yelled Grandpa.

There was a puff of wind — and he was gone. As he sailed out over the lake, his voice came floating back. "Oh, off we go, into the wild blue yonder . . ."

The singing grew faint as the red wings soared higher. The figure hanging beneath them grew smaller and smaller. As Morris watched anxiously, the hang-glider made a sort of circle over the water and then turned back towards shore. Morris heaved a sigh of relief.

But instead of heading inland towards the bean patch, his grandfather seemed to be drifting farther away — along the shore of the lake!

He was above the trees, but only just. "GRAMPS!" shouted Morris. "YOU'RE GOING THE WRONG WAY!"

But there was no answer. The Wings of Icarus slowly disappeared behind a hill.

Morris paced up and down, waiting for his grandfather to reappear. Shielding his eyes from the sun, he scanned the sky.

He looked at his watch. It was quarter to ten! He ran back across the field to the house. Fireweed raised her head and looked at him curiously as he raced past the pasture. When he reached the fence, he stood on the middle rail and surveyed the old bean field.

There was no sign of his grandfather, or the glider. Something was very wrong!

If I only had my bike here, thought Morris, *I could go and look for him.*

Then he noticed Fireweed grazing in the pasture.

If she has her halter on, maybe I could ride her.

He raced to the barn, but Fireweed's halter was still hanging there. So was the bridle. Grandpa had said Fireweed needed a bit and bridle to control her . . .

Quickly Morris made up his mind. Grabbing the bridle and reins, he ran to the pasture.

Fireweed watched him coming. When he got

near, she strolled away, cropping grass as she went.

"Fireweed, COME!" yelled Morris desperately. But the big grey horse just swished her tail and kept moving away.

Morris raced back to the barn and got a handful of oats.

This time he was successful. While Fireweed munched the oats, he slipped the bit into her mouth and pulled the bridle over her head.

Leading her to the gate, he opened it. He climbed up on the rails and hoisted himself onto her back.

"Come on, Fireweed. Let's go!" he cried, nudging her fat sides with his feet.

But she just stood there. Morris leaned forward and patted her neck. "Fireweed, Gramps is out there somewhere, and I'm afraid he's in trouble. He's got nobody to help him but you and me. We've got to find him!"

Morris never knew if it was what he said to Fireweed or if it was the extra little kick he gave her with his heels, but she suddenly began to move out.

Just to be on the safe side, he kept hold of a handful of her mane as he guided her across the field. As they followed a path along the top of the cliff, he scanned the sky above and the water below. But except for some crows circling noisily above the trees in the distance, he saw nothing.

He had to keep looking. What if his grandfather was hanging in a tree somewhere?!

"GRANDPA!" he hollered. "WHERE ARE YOU?"

There was no answer.

Morris rode on. Then, at the top of a little rise, Fireweed paused. For a brief moment Morris thought he glimpsed something red in the field below, but he wasn't sure.

"GRAMPS!" he shouted. Fireweed lifted her head, sniffing the air. Then she whinnied — a high, shrill, trumpeting call.

The sound sent shivers down Morris's spine. "Good girl!" he cried. "You'll help me find him, won't you?"

But Fireweed stood frozen in her tracks. Her nostrils quivered, and she stared ahead. Suddenly she turned, and the next minute they were plunging off the trail into the trees.

"WHOA! WHOA! STOP! ARRETE!" yelled Morris, hanging on for all he was worth.

Finally Fireweed slowed down, and Morris turned around to see what had frightened her. There, on the trail they had just left, was a huge brown bear with two cubs.

"Oh, man! Let's get out of here!" cried Morris.

They trotted on, and as they passed near the edge of the cliff, Morris looked down at the lake. There in a little cove, tied to an old root, was the boat with the fishing poles. But there was no one in it.

Those guys don't seem to be doing much fishing, he thought.

It was then that he heard a faint voice crying, "MAYDAY! MAYDAY!"

15

"Grandpa? Is that you?" Morris called.

"Sssshhh!" hissed the voice. "I'm over here!"

Sliding off Fireweed's back, Morris sneaked around behind the stump. There was Grandpa, sitting on the ground, tied to a tree with yellow rope. His new overalls were torn, and his flying helmet was tilted over one eye.

"Gramps! What happened?"

"Poachers!" spluttered his grandfather. "Miserable miscreants! Villains! Sleaze balls! They robbed the nest!"

"Charles and Diana's?" croaked Morris.

"Took the fledglings right out of it!"

"Oh, no! That means the Baghdad bazaar for them! Where are they? I've got to find them!"

"Help untie me, first," said Grandpa. "And keep your voice down!"

"Why?" asked Morris as he struggled with the knots.

"Because the poachers are still around!" hissed his grandfather. "I heard them say they

92

were going to wait until dark before they leave. I think they've gone down to the beach."

"How come they tied you up like this?"

"While I was flying around, I saw something going on around the nest, so I floated over to investigate. You were right about that boat we saw, by the way. Those fishing poles were just camouflage. Anyway, I caught them red-handed, putting the fledglings into a gunny sack. They saw me watching, so they shot me down. Blasted a hole right through my left wing, the miserable miscreants!"

Morris looked nervously over his shoulder. "Gunny sack? Gramps, was one of them the man we saw in the hardware store? The one with the icicle eyes?"

"Come to think of it, it was. Gimlet-eyed, I call him! He's wearing a black leather coat and two pairs of binoculars. He's a mean one, all right! And I was the one who told him where to get his gunny sack!"

I knew it! thought Morris. *I knew that guy was bad news!* As he released the rope, his grandfather leaned forward and rubbed his ankle.

"What's the matter, Gramps? Is your ankle broken?"

"I think it's just strained," replied Grandpa as he struggled to his feet.

"Where's your hang-glider now?"

"Right over there in the clearing. You should have seen me come spinning down, Morris! Kazooie, kazooie, kaZAMM! Anyway, we'd better get back to the house and notify the R.C.M.P. They can be waiting for the poachers when they get to Cranberry Corners."

"But what if the poachers go somewhere else?"

"Hmmm. Hadn't thought of that."

"Gramps, I've got an idea. I know where their boat is. I saw it when I was coming to find you. Why don't I sneak down to the lake and untie it? Then the poachers can't go anywhere."

Grandpa shook his head. "Good idea, but too risky for you. I'll do it."

"But you can't with your sore ankle! They won't see me. I'll be really careful. Then the Mounties can come in their police boat and catch them and rescue the baby falcons. Maybe I can even rescue them right now!"

"That's no good," said Grandpa. "They have to catch these poachers with the goods. And how are the police going to find this place from the water if the boat's gone?"

Morris looked thoughtful. Suddenly he cried, "The Wings of Icarus! They're nice and bright.

Lean them up against a tree, and they can be the marker!"

"Hmmm. Might work . . ."

"Then we'll ride home on Fireweed and phone the Mounties. We have to do it, Gramps! For the falcons!"

"All right," said Grandpa. "For the falcons!"

While his grandfather tethered Fireweed back from the edge of the cliff, Morris began to pick his way down the bank in the direction of the cove.

He was sweating in the hot sun as he crept along, keeping low behind the huckleberry bushes. Once his foot slipped, sending a stone rolling down ahead of him. Morris's heart flew into his mouth, and for a few minutes he huddled there, afraid to move.

But he didn't hear anything. Finally he decided it was safe to continue, and once again he began stealthily picking his way down. At last, hot and dusty, he scrambled out onto the gravelly beach. There, just a little piece away, he saw the boat. Tied to a big root on the shore, it was bobbing gently up and down in the water.

But then Morris groaned. For just beyond the old root, sitting in the shade of a big maple tree, were two men. Beside them, tied with a piece of yellow rope, was a gunny sack.

The men were eating bananas and talking. One of them Morris had never seen before, but the other he recognized instantly. It was old Icicle Eyes himself!

Suddenly Morris saw him put binoculars up to his eyes and scan the beach. Quaking in his boots, he huddled behind a bush, waiting.

Seemingly satisfied with what he saw, Icicle Eyes lay down, putting his hat over his eyes. Soon the other man stretched out as well.

Now's my chance! thought Morris. He crept forward and untied the boat. Giving it a push with his foot, he watched it slowly float away. He looked up the cliff and saw a bold red marker in the trees. Grandpa had put the Wings of Icarus where they could not be missed!

He scrambled back up the bank as silently and as quickly as he could.

"Well done!" said Grandpa, when he reached the top. "Now, let's get going. Every minute counts!" He heaved himself onto Fireweed's broad back, then pulled Morris up behind him.

Just as they started to leave, there was a rustle of wings, and two shadows passed over the treetops.

"It's Charles and Diana!" cried Morris.

Then they heard it. A dreadful, wailing cry.

"They've found the babies gone from the nest," said Grandpa.

"Can't we go any faster?" begged Morris.

At that moment, Fireweed lifted her head. Her ears pricked forward and her nostrils quivered. She began to trot.

"Here we go!" cried Morris, tightening his grip on Grandpa's overalls. "Fireweed smells the barn!"

16

With the cries of the falcons ringing in their ears, Morris and Grandpa Rumpel rode home.

At last Fireweed loped into the paddock, where she headed straight for her bathtub of water.

"You run right in and get the police number for me," Grandpa told Morris as he carefully lowered himself from Fireweed's back.

As he hobbled into the kitchen, he was rubbing his hip and mumbling, "Oy! That was one tough ride!"

"I got the police number!" Morris handed his grandfather the phone. Then he stood listening anxiously while Grandpa Rumpel made his report.

"They're coming right away," said Grandpa, hanging up the phone. "And they're bringing a conservation officer with them."

"Oh, whew!" sighed Morris, wiping his brow. "What a relief!" Suddenly he felt hungry. Ravenous, in fact. "Hey, we missed lunch! And what about Fireweed? She must be really hungry! Can I feed her some hay?"

"Yes. But give her a good rub-down first. She really needs it after that ride."

As Morris went into the barn to get the old towel they used for rubbing down, he felt a heavy weight on his shoulder. He looked around, and there was Fireweed, resting her head on him as she followed him in.

"Fireweed, you old phoney. I think you like me, after all. I just wish everybody could know what you did! Did you know you saved the falcons?"

When he got back to the house, his grandfather had set out some homemade bread, cheese, two large tomatoes and a carton of milk. In the middle of the table was the remainder of Morris's lemon pie.

"I thought we might as well eat it before it went all funny," explained Grandpa.

"Sure! I'd forgotten all about the pies!"

Just as they were finishing lunch, Grandpa said, "Sssshhh! Listen!"

"A boat!" Jumping up, Morris ran over to the window.

Grandpa Rumpel got the binoculars and focussed them on the lake below. "It's the R.C.M.P. patrol boat. They're on their way."

"YIPPEE! How about if we take the truck and go down there, too?"

"No, we'd only be in the way. The police don't want any interference at this stage. Don't forget, those men are armed! The corporal said he'd let us know when they had them safely in custody."

"I guess the conservation office will put the babies back in the nest, huh?"

"I imagine so. If they're all right."

"Does he get paid for looking after wild animals and birds?"

"Right."

A gleam came into Morris's eyes. "Maybe that's what I'll be when I grow up. A conservation officer!"

"Not a flier? A pilot, like your old grandpa?"

"Well, maybe that, too. But I'd like to look after baby birds and stuff. I'll probably fly a hang-glider, too — in my spare time."

His grandfather nodded. "You know," he said, "all things considered, that wasn't a bad flight today. Even my crash landing was done with a certain amount of finesse."

* * *

While they waited for the call from the police,

Grandpa stretched out on the chesterfield and dozed off. Morris studied his bird book.

After a while, he heard the sound of a motor down on the lake. "They're coming back, Gramps!" he cried.

"I'll never be the same again!" groaned Grandpa, heaving himself up into a sitting position and stuffing a pillow under his seat. "Have they got the poachers?"

"I can't tell. They've gone around the corner. But here comes somebody up the driveway."

It was Grandma, driving up in a cloud of dust. "Thank goodness you're here!" she cried, running into the house, her black nun's robes flapping behind her. "There's a rumour in town about some poachers. They say somebody got shot! The Mounties went out to look for them!" Breathless, she collapsed into her swivel rocker.

"It was Grandpa!" shouted Morris. "The poachers shot Grandpa down and poached the eggs . . . I mean, the babies!"

"Oh, Erasmus! Where did they get you?" Jumping out of her chair, Grandma flitted over to his side. Seeing the look of anguish on his face as he sat there on his cushion, she cried out, "Not . . . not your sit-upon?"

"No, no," protested Grandpa. "Morris and I had a long, hard ride on Fireweed, that's all."

"Don't forget your ankle, Grandpa," added Morris.

And together they filled her in on the day's adventures.

Just as they finished, the phone rang. With Morris and Grandma hanging over his shoulder, Grandpa listened while the police brought him up to date. At last he hung up the receiver and turned to them, beaming.

"It's all over! The fledglings are safely back in the nest, and the poachers are in custody!"

"YAHOOO!" shouted Morris and Grandma.

"And they're very grateful for our assistance."

"They're welcome!" said Morris.

"Now let's take the truck and collect the Wings of Icarus. I want to get them mended tonight."

* * *

At last the long day ended. As Grandpa hobbled upstairs to bed with the hot-water bottle,

Grandma asked, "What's that you've got under your arm?"

"Nothing," he mumbled.

"I saw it," piped up Morris. "It's the saddle catalogue."

17

It was breakfast time a few days later. Grandpa was almost as good as new, though not quite.

"I just need some good solid food, that's all," he said, sitting down on the two pillows he had carefully arranged on his chair.

"Maybe now we'll get a saddle," said Grandma, putting a platter of pancakes on the table.

"I was thinking the same thing," said Grandpa. "After all, you've wanted one for a long time."

"Fireweed was a real hero the other day, wasn't she?" Morris said as he reached for the blueberry syrup.

His grandmother gave him a hug. "From what I hear, you were the hero!"

"He was, indeed!" said Grandpa, smothering his pancakes with butter and syrup. "Even had I been able to extricate myself from my —"

"Not so much butter, Erasmus," interrupted Grandma. "Remember what the —"

"I know, I know!" said Grandpa peevishly. "As I was saying — even had I been able to extricate myself from my predicament, I would have been unable to save the falcons!" Taking a large bite of pancake, he made a face. "These pancakes taste . . . uh . . . sort of different."

"It's a new recipe," Grandma told him. "I invented it myself. They're called Good-for-You Pancakes. They've got wheat germ, oat bran and goat's milk in them."

"Yuck," said Morris quietly.

After breakfast, Grandpa headed out to his workshop. "Are you coming, Morris?" he called. "We have to check on my wings to see if the fabric mender worked."

"Right on!" said Morris, following him outside.

Grandma decided to relax after the strenuous last few days of Grandpa's recuperation. Pouring herself another cup of coffee, she went into the living-room and flopped down on the chesterfield. With a happy sigh, she kicked off her slippers and opened the paper.

She had almost finished reading it when she heard the car. *Beep-be-beep-beep! Beep-be-beep-beep!* — all the way up the driveway.

"It's Harvey!" she cried. Hitching up her dressing-gown and tripping over her slippers, she hurried to the door. She rushed outside and was nearly bowled over by Snowflake, who was looking for Rocket. He hurtled past, shedding long white hairs and bits of woolly undercoat as he went.

Following Snowflake came Quincy and Leah — all arms and legs in their tie-dyed shorts. "Grandma!" they cried, rushing at her with arms outstretched, and nearly bowling her over again.

"You're looking good, Mom," said Mr. Rumpel, giving his mother a bear hug.

"I'd have looked better if I'd known you were coming today!" gasped Grandma, trying to fluff up her hair.

"But I told Morris on the phone," said Mrs. Rumpel. "Didn't he tell you?"

Just then, Morris himself came running around the corner of the house. "Yo, family!" he greeted them breezily. "I thought I heard the old set of wheels!"

"Morris!" cried his mother. "What happened to your hair?"

"It's okay, Mom. I've still got it. Al saved it for me in a Baggie."

"This boy is a real hero!" said Grandma. "Just wait until you hear about it!"

"What happened?" cried all the Rumpels.

"I just rode Fireweed bareback and rescued Gramps after the poachers shot him down, and then I set their boat adrift and the police caught them and we saved the falcons!" said Morris.

"I don't believe it!" scoffed Quincy. "You can't even ride. You're making it up!"

"I can so! I am not!"

"Are you all right?" cried his mother, feeling his forehead. "They didn't hurt you, did they?"

"I'm glad all that didn't happen to me." Leah shivered just thinking about it.

"I always knew Morris had it in him!" Mr. Rumpel beamed proudly at his son.

Suddenly Leah said, "Look!" And she pointed to the sky.

"It's Charles and Diana!" cried Morris. "And they've got their babies with them!"

With rapid beats of their slender striped wings, the four falcons flew over the house.

"Wow!" exclaimed the Rumpels.

As the birds disappeared from sight, another airborne object came floating into view.

"What's that?" cried Quincy.

The airborne object came closer. Now they could see the red hang-glider with a bright-yellow patch on one wing. Suspended beneath it was a figure in striped overalls and an old-fashioned flying helmet.

"It's Grandpa!"

As he swooped over them, Grandpa gave a little wave. Then, grasping his controls confidently, he swooped away towards the bean patch.

"Grandpa and the Wings of Icarus!" said Morris proudly.

THE END

Other books by Betty Waterton

Quincy Rumpel

Quincy Rumpel wants pierced ears, curly hair and a Save-the-Whales T-shirt.

Her sister, Leah, can't see why she shouldn't have pierced ears, too, while Morris, her brother, longs for a dog.

Mrs. Rumpel hopes for rain, so her job at the umbrella shop will thrive.

And the neighbours, the Murphys, just can't decide whether having the Rumpels next door is the best or the worst thing that ever happened to them.

ISBN 0-88899-036-7 $5.95   paperback

Starring Quincy Rumpel

About to enter grade seven, Quincy Rumpel is determined that this is the year she will make her mark on the world and become a star. As Mr. Rumpel tries to market his latest business venture, the Rumpel Rebounders, Quincy embarks on a grand plan to advertise the rebounders on television and ensure stardom for herself at the same time.

In this sequel to the enormously popular *Quincy Rumpel,* the whole eccentric clan is back in the rambling house at 57 Tulip Street — Leah, Morris, Mr. and Mrs. Rumpel, cousin Gwen and the Murphys. They are joined by crazy Auntie Fan Twistle and Quincy's latest heart-throb, Morris's soccer coach, Desmond.

ISBN 0-88899-048-0 $5.95   paperback

Quincy Rumpel, P.I.

Why is Quincy Rumpel creeping around the old Beanblossom house? Has she discovered the bizarre burial ground of the little dog, Nanki-poo? And what are the strange apparitions that her brother, Morris, sees in the house at night? How about the treasure that Captain Beanblossom left behind? And, most important, who else is interested in the abandoned house?

Quincy Rumpel is back again with an all-woman private investigating firm. But her best-laid plans soon go astray when she's joined by ever-bothersome Morris, his best friend, Chucky, and her heart-throb, Freddie Twikenham, who is convinced that he has his grandfather's Mountie blood coursing through his veins.

ISBN 0-88899-081-2 $5.95   paperback